Animals

Monke

by Nick Rebman

FOCUS READERS

FOCUS READERS

www.focusreaders.com

Focus Readers is distributed by North Star Editions:
sales@northstareditions.com | 888-417-0195

Produced for Focus Readers by Red Line Editorial.

Photographs ©: Ondrej Prosicky/Shutterstock Images, cover, 1; Cuson/Shutterstock Images, 4 (top); DibaniMedia/Shutterstock Images, 4 (bottom); LeonP/Shutterstock Images, 7; Red ivory/Shutterstock Images, 9, 16 (bottom left); Sergey Uryadnikov/Shutterstock Images, 11; luckyraccoon/Shutterstock Images, 13; Anton_Ivanov/Shutterstock Images, 15; lining/Shutterstock Images, 16 (top left); Artem Samokhvalov/Shutterstock Images, 16 (top right); Max Lashcheuski/Shutterstock Images, 16 (bottom right)

ISBN
978-1-63517-852-4 (hardcover)
978-1-63517-953-8 (paperback)
978-1-64185-156-5 (ebook pdf)
978-1-64185-055-1 (hosted ebook)

Library of Congress Control Number: 2018931101

Printed in the United States of America
Mankato, MN
May, 2018

About the Author

Nick Rebman enjoys reading, drawing, and traveling to places where he doesn't speak the language. He lives in Minnesota.

Table of Contents

Monkeys

There are many kinds
of monkeys.
Some are small.
Some are big.

A monkey has two arms.

A monkey has two legs.

A monkey has a tail.

tail
leg
arm

Behavior

Monkeys can **hang**.

Monkeys can yell.

Monkeys can play.

Monkeys live
in groups.
Most monkeys live
in trees.

Food

Some monkeys eat **fruit**.

Some monkeys eat **nuts**.

Some monkeys eat **seeds**.

fruit

Monkeys are smart.
Some live for 15 years.
Some live for 40 years
or more.

Glossary

fruit

nuts

hang

seeds

Index